BEAR
NEEDS
HELP

Sarah S. Brannen

Philomel Books

PHILOMEL BOOKS
an imprint of Penguin Random House LLC
375 Hudson Street, New York, NY 10014

Library of Congress Cataloging-in-Publication Data
Names: Brannen, Sarah S., author, illustrator. | Title: Bear needs help / Sarah S. Brannen.
Description: New York, NY : Philomel Books, [2019] | Summary: A young bear needs help with an untied shoe. | Identifiers: LCCN 2017039495 |
ISBN 9780525516507 (hardcover) | ISBN 9780525516538 (e-book) | Subjects: | CYAC: Shoelaces—Fiction. | Shoes—Fiction. | Bears—Fiction. |
Classification: LCC PZ7.B737514 Be 2019 | DDC [E]—dc23 | LC record available at https://lccn.loc.gov/2017039495

Manufactured in China by RR Donnelley Asia Printing Solutions Ltd.
ISBN 9780525516507
1 3 5 7 9 10 8 6 4 2

Edited by Talia Benamy.   Design by Jennifer Chung.   Text set in Caecilia LT Pro.
The art was done in watercolor on 300 lb. Arches Bright White cold press paper.

To Steven Chudney,
who gave Bear so much help.

Oh no.

Excuse me . . .

Pardon me . . .

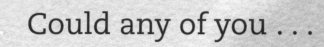

Could any of you . . .

help me . . . ?

Oh dear.

Shoelaces again?

Yup.

Thank you!

He really needs to learn to do that himself.

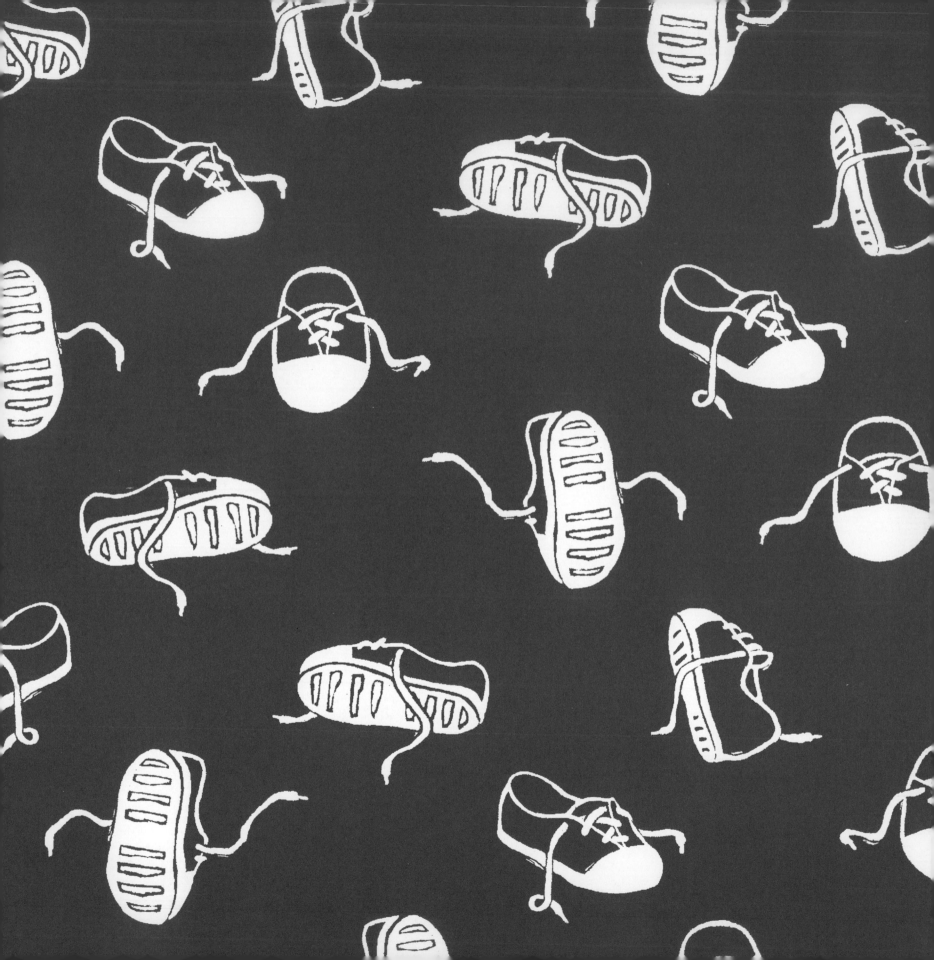